Twisted Realities
A collection of horror
This is a work of fiction. The characters, incidents, and dialogue are all drawn from the author's imagination and are not to be construed as real. Any resemblance to actual events or persons, living or dead, is entirely coincidental.

Twisted Realities A collection of Horror © 2024 by Camille Danciu. All rights reserved. Printed in the United States of America. No part of this book may be used or reproduced in any manner whatsoever without written permission except in the case of brief quotations embodied in critical articles and reviews.

Imprint: Independently published
ISBN: 9798334639614
Cover Art by: Rooster Republic Press
Visit Roosterrepublicpress.com for more cover designs.

Twisted Realities

A collection of horror

Camille Danciu

Contents

The Sewer Flies 1

Busy Beaver …………..13

Alternate Addict ……....20

Area 69 ………………..36

Mirror Mirror …………48

The Attic……………….72

How do you know if you're paranoid?

When you feel like you're being watched or listened to, is it paranoia?

Or is it a biological response to real stimuli for self-preservation?

THE SEWER FLIES

There was a fresh one every morning. Every time Heidi leaned her head back to rinse the suds from her hair, her eyes landed on a new sewer fly. Same spot. Every morning. Lather, rinse, repeat.

Jesus Christ. She thought to herself as she slapped the fly down with her washcloth. As the sewer fly landed in the tub, it caught Heidi's eye.

What the hell.

Bending down to get a better look she saw a quick flash. Something was flashing on its back. Using a piece of toilet paper, she collected the wet fly carcass.

There it was again!

It kept flashing. Toweling herself off in the bathroom and trying to rush herself out the door before the thing stopped flashing. She wanted to bring this fly to the computer store. Figuring that was a good as place as any to start.

This could be it!

Having just been sent on a paid leave at work she had nothing but time to think and dig around her house for wires and bugs. Although not sure why she would be the subject of someone's wiring or bugging to begin with.

Wasn't that for major criminals? I haven't done anything.

Imagining she looked like a mental patient disassembling her light fixtures and searching for hidden cameras. It gave her great satisfaction finding this fly. Like she was right all along. Suspicions confirmed.

This all started when a picture of her naked body in the shower appeared in the middle of her presentation at work. All her colleagues were in attendance. Needless to say, she embarrassed not only herself, but the firm as well.

Stumbling upon actual evidence of a possible crime would certainly vindicate her at work. Would it save her reputation? Probably not. Would the men at work still ogle her based on the bird's eye view from her shower where this very specimen was just killed? Absolutely.

Screw it. It's worth a shot.

The computer shop was a two-minute drive from her house. It was situated between two larger establishments. Quaint and a little rundown. Being that it was not a big box store she hoped for sympathy and personal connection.

Perfect.

Opening the door jingled a small chime over her head to the back of the building. Waiting in the center of the shop with the toilet paper in her hand, Heidi began to look around the store. She was alone.

They'll probably think I'm crazy.

"Hello, welcome to Comp Geeks. I'm Cedrik, what can I do for you today?

He was tall with dark hair and dark eyes. Wearing a suit that seemed too serious and formal for a computer repair shop.

Uh oh. Hopefully he's not as tight up as that suit.

"Hi. I have an odd request. I found *this* in my bathroom." She passed the piece of toilet paper across the glass counter. "I know how this looks. I had a situation a work where a picture of me naked showed up in my presentation. And no, I didn't put it there. Anyway, it was the same angle where I found this. It has a flashing light on it. I figured I'd come here first because it might be a chip or something computer related."

"Like a spying device?" He asked.

Cedrik had already taken out a magnifying glass and leaned over it.

Slowly looking over the magnifying glass, he stared at Heidi.

Oh no, he thinks I'm crazy.

"This is incredible." He stated. "I've never seen a computer chip so small. And you think it's capable of taking pictures?" He asked genuinely interested.

Not sure she was happy to be on the receiving end of the awe-inspiring revelation Cedrik was having, she was grateful he saw it too, nonetheless.

"Yea I'm pretty sure this is the source of the picture. I mean, it only makes sense. It's the same angle. I certainly wouldn't take a picture of myself and put it in the middle of my own presentation."

"I can try to see if I can pull any information off it for you. Have you been to this shop before?" Cedrik asked.

"I don't know, maybe. It's been years."

"Tell me your name and I'll see if you're in the system so I can give you a call when I'm done."

"Heidi Cole."

He typed away at his computer.

"Ah, I gotcha. Heidi Cole, you haven't been to visit the shop in 3 years. Confirm the number you're using please?"

Rattling off her cellphone number and email, she felt relieved that he would help her.

"Okay, I'll give you a call if I can pull something off this thing. In the meantime, maybe you should stay at a hotel or something. I doubt these things came from the sewer. It might not be safe at your place." He suggested.

"You're right."

Luckily for Heidi, there was a decent hotel just a few minutes from her house. She could check on her place daily. Sleeping there was out of the question. There was nothing scarier than the thought of being dead asleep and waking up to some creep hovering over her in the pitch black.

She shuddered. *This is bad.*

Using her cellphone, she booked the hotel room while sitting in her car out front of her house. Feeling unsafe for the first time in life. Gathering clothes from inside looked like a tornado spun through. She ripped through closets and draws, then scurried out with one full backpack.

While checking in at the front desk, she overheard a couple talking about the dinner specials at the hotel bar. That's just what she needed. A night off from cooking and socializing.

Win-win.

The dinner dress she picked out complemented her skin and hair perfectly. Sage green. Her strawberry blond hair fell to the middle of her back and the straps of the dress accentuated her freckles.

The freckles that my whole company got to see. She thought while admiring the back of the dress in the mirror.

The hotel dining room was packed. It was bound to be good with a crowd this large. Finding a small table for two in the corner, she started looking over the menu.

Before she had a chance to order, Cedrik plopped down in front of her.

"Oh my gosh what're you doing here Cedrik?"

"I needed to talk to you and when you told me where you'd be staying, I was familiar with the area."

Did I tell him where I planned to stay?

"Look, I pulled some information from the chip. Everything suggests that this connection came from your home Wi-Fi."

"How do you know that?"

How could he know my home Wi-Fi?

He turned his phone around. "Heidi Home" was written on the screen.

"Oh, yeah, I forgot I named it. Duh." She said blushing.

"Don't be embarrassed. It's a scary time for you."

"What do I do then? Do I have enough evidence to go to the police?"

"I don't know but if you want me to take you to the police and back up your story maybe this is enough evidence to open an investigation. I bet they have a specialist for this sort of thing."

"Alright then what're we waiting for?" Heidi began packing up her purse.

"You want to go right now?"

"Yes."

"I'll drive you. I'm parked out back."

Cedrik followed Heidi to the back of the building.

"That's me right there." Cedrik said flashing his car's lights with his keys.

Heidi climbed in the passenger seat. They drove silently towards the police station. Or what Heidi assumed was the police station. She had never been there. Cedrik turned a couple times and pulled up behind a warehouse type building.

"Cedrik where are we?"

He grabbed ahold of her from behind wrapping a cloth over her mouth.

"Shh."

Her vision faded out away from her as the world went black and quiet.

Sounds came whooshing into her ears and her vision was coming back to her. Foggy and unclear. Pulling herself up she looked around. This was an unfamiliar room.

Smelling bacon and toasted bread, she became confused.

Am I delirious?

Her legs felt like two lead weights. Massaging them and slapping them a little made the feeling come back. Standing slowly and making her way to the door in the room, she was shocked to discover it was unlocked.

Weird.

When she opened the door, she saw short hallway and a staircase. Realizing she had been changed out of her dinner dress, she became scared.

The smells of the bacon were more intense now. She could hear the pots and pans rattling. It sounded like a Saturday morning. Except this was anything but.

"Hello?" She called out weakly.

Nothing.

She continued to scoot down the stairs cautiously on her butt. Upon getting to the bottom, she saw a front door that was chained up. The hallway led to a kitchen. Assuming that is where the bacon smell was originating, she followed her nose.

As she rounded the corner into the kitchen, she let out an audible gasp.

"Cedrik."

He twirled around shirtless with a towel over his shoulder. Saying nothing, just staring at her.

"It was you. The sewer flies, the picture at work. You stalked me to my hotel too."

"No, I watched as you booked it through the software I installed. There's a difference. Technology takes talent, stalking is just creepy."

"The picture at my job. Why? Please let me go. My boyfriend will be looking for me."

"Oh Heidi. You don't think I already know about your love life? I've watched you for months. The flies, the picture, I hacked into the computer and rigged the search engine to show my computer shop. You really think I don't know that you're single. You have been for 823 days too."

"Why are you doing this?" She cried.

"I'm on the verge of a technological breakthrough." He said as he grabbed her.

Spinning her around and pinning her to the floor, he poked her finger with a needle. Using a device she had never seen before, he collected the droplets of blood. The blood-filled device was then inserted into a computer the size of an entire wall in his kitchen.

"What the hell is going on?"

A whirring noise and some short beeps followed. As she sat on the floor gathering herself, a series of holograms started forming in static patterns on the floor. The feet first, then the calves and thighs.

Oh my God, they're bodies.

Three women materialized in front of her. All strawberry blondes. All with freckles. There, at the end of the row... she was looking herself in the eyes. Cedrik came up behind her and wrapped her head with a plastic bag.

As Heidi flailed in front of the Heidi hologram suffocating, all four of the holographic women said in unison, "Hello Cedrik."

Cedrik dropped the physical body of Heidi and admired his collection.

"Still some bugs to iron out, but I'm close." He said smiling at his ladies.

Why do they say, "busy beaver?"
Where'd that come from anyway?

Busy Beavers

For weeks Brian heard the gnawing. It kept him up at night. The twigs snapping and breaking had become the white noise to his sleepless nights.

Living close to a stream and large wooded area, he knew the wildlife would be busy, but this was over the top.

What the hell are those beavers building? A damn apartment complex?

Thinking the beavers were probably more efficient than contractors, he wanted to look at their construction.

Tomorrow. He thought to himself as he settled into his bed to try to get some sleep.

The next morning, with his coffee in hand, Brian went into his backyard. The stream met his yard about fifty feet away from his house.

Walking upstream, he kept his eyes peeled for the dam and beaver motel he suspected was being built.

It was huge. He could see why they were so busy. The dam looked like the size of his entire kitchen. He had never seen a dam that big.

No wonder they're doing all that gnawing.

As Brian turned to walk away, he thought he heard a muffled groan. Whipping his head back around towards the dam, he saw nothing.

I'm spending too much time alone.

Having retired a year ago Brian had ample time on his hands. He'd spent most of his days napping and taking the occasional walk on his desolate street.

Having drank the last of his coffee, he shrugged it off and went back inside. The chill in the air was biting at his ears already.

Brian's dinners were spent alone. His dog passed away years ago and he didn't have the heart to replace him. It felt wrong.

During dinner he heard a muffled scream. Setting his fork down, he decided to take his evening walk early.

What in the world is that?

There it was again. The gnawing. The beavers were busy again.

Do they ever stop?

His road was mostly loose stone and gravel. The crunching beneath his feet did nothing to muddle the occasional scream. The scream was growing lower. Wondering if someone was hurt, he began following the scream.

Following his ears led him from the gravel street to the bank of the stream. Slowly but surely his house came back into view as he passed through the trees. He crossed over the stream where a log had fallen. Being careful to jump from the log to exposed rocks. The last thing he needed was soaked feet in this cold.

A muffled scream came again. He stood completely still staring around the woods. Blood.

Shit.

He turned around in circles thinking a predator was behind him sneaking up. Nothing.

Following the blood drips and splatters, he was alarmed when the blood ended in the stream. Perplexed, he stood there for a minute.

Then, he saw the huge beaver dam. The scream was so muffled and weak he almost couldn't hear it anymore.

From in there? My gosh.

Having only dressed for a walk he didn't want to risk freezing to death jumping in the cold water without preparation. He would have to come back tomorrow.

That night the gnawing was even worse. The screams had subsided. He began to wonder if he was at the age where old people lose their wits.

64 is too young to be losing it.

The entire night was gnawing, tossing, turning, and yawning. As the sun came up to greet him, he skipped the coffee and went to his garage for a flashlight, machete, and an old wetsuit he used for his deep-sea fishing trips back in the day. It was snug now around his potbelly.

Today I'm going to get to the bottom of this.

He stalked back out into his back yard with the sun high above his head. Making his way to the dam again, he heard nothing. Not even one scream today.

Crossing the stream again he made his way to the back of the beaver dam. He placed his ear as close to the branches and logs as he could get. Nothing. Not even a peep.

Maybe they're semi-nocturnal.

He used his hands and the machete to try to make his way into the dam. The logs were too thick and sturdy. He'd be standing there forever hacking away. Fearing he would have to enter the way the beavers did, he came prepared.

He grabbed his flashlight and zipped it in a Ziploc bag while he plunged into the water. Hoping to shield the flashlight from the water, he swam quickly to the bottom of the dam.

His hands and face were frozen. Trembling, he found the opening to the dam. Just in time. He thought for a second he was going to run out of breath.

His head popped up in the opening of the dam. It was empty as far as he could see. He pulled himself inside and unwrapped the flashlight.

Flicking the flashlight on, nothing happened. He slapped it a couple time into his palm. It flickered on. Spinning around in a circle on his knees, he came across the badly mutilated remains of a small woman. Her stomach was chewed apart and her legs were hacked up badly.

Jesus Christ. He gagged into the crook of his arm.

He crawled over to the body.

"Hello?" He called out while gently feeling for her pulse.

Slap

The slapping of the beaver's tail jolted him from the body. There was no pulse.

I gotta get out of here!

He crawled back to the entrance of the dam just to be faced with an abnormally large beaver poking its head up staring at him. Now clawing its way back into his dam. Shining the flashlight around, he found a corridor in the circle.

Crouching all the way down he wormed his way down the corridor of sticks and logs into another round den. His flashlight died halfway through.

Just great.

He could hear the beaver coming from behind him. Bashing his flashlight into his palm, it flickered to life.

He was confronted with five of the fattest, biggest beavers he'd ever seen. Behind the beavers was a pile of mutilated, pulpy human bodies.

Holy shit.

Taking his flashlight into his hand above his head he began to swing at the beavers. He was no match for the claws, teeth, and tails.

Brian was attacked, being bitten, and clawed. Not dead but certainly well on his way. He lay in the corner of the extended den surrounded by rotting corpses.

No wonder they call them busy beavers.

"They'll say anything to save their own skin…"
But which skin are they saving?

Alternate Addict

"Get him!" Shouted the officer. "He's coming out your side!"

Brandon was barreling through the alley way. His shoes slamming into the oily puddles. Each puddle saturating his holey shoes. His feet felt like he contracted a case of trench foot. He knew they stunk.

Charging the gate in front of him, desperate to get away. He flung himself onto it without hesitation. Gripping the fence with his fingers spread wide he began to climb. Weighed down by five pounds of wet clothes made the task that much more difficult.

When he got to the top of the gate, he tossed himself onto the dumpster lid below. He fell right through. The stench of the dumpster assaulted his nose immediately.

Smelling, and drenched from the knees down, he slid into the smallest crevice in the alleyway. Listening. Stifling the urge to kneel over and heave, he grabbed his mouth. Stopping himself from being loud, he listened and couldn't hear anything. Silence.

He slid down the brick wall. His shirt catching and snagging on the bricks all the way down. Scraping his back. Sitting and catching his breath before attempting to leave the crevice.

Feeling confident that the officers had given up their chase, he walked gingerly to the front of the crevice that led out to the main alleyway.

Folding up his pants and turning them into long shorts, in an attempt to hide the obvious wetness from the puddles. He adjusted his collar and regained his usual strut and set out on the pavement again. Knowing the street would be a last resort to emerge, he began testing door handles to see if any careless workers had left them unlocked. He had terrible luck.

None of the doors were open so he had no choice but to come out the other side of the alley way. Certain the police would be there to tackle him, he braced himself for impact upon emerging on the street.

When no tackle came, he let his guard down just a bit. Operating at his usual pace, he continued walking. He did not check behind him or look around, knowing how unnatural and suspicious that made people look.

Act natural.

Tires screeched and radios beeped. They had two cars now. Surrounding him and jumping out. Four of them were on him now.

Gosh all this for me. He thought to himself.

He started sweating. Thinking about how smelly his feet would be in jail, he made another attempt at evasion.

The cop had his hand on the back of his collar in two seconds. He was not getting out of it this time.

"You're under arrest Brandon." The officer said as he continued and read off his rights.

"Listen, I can give up much more important people than me. You know, the ones in charge of bringing this stuff in." Brandon said desperately.

"They'll say anything to save their own skin." The arresting officer said to his partner as he lowered Brandon's head and squished him in the back of the cruiser.

The door slammed. All Brandon could do with lay his head on the door and kick his shoes off. Rerunning the situation through his mind a few times. Regretful of his ignorance to see the patrol car right behind him while he was scoring his stuff.

If only I had gone inside the house to cop. He thought regretfully.

Feeling stupid and ashamed he buried his head as far as he could in his scrunched-up knees while he took the trip downtown.

Arriving in the county jail was different than being in the holding cell. Brandon expected not to be let off the hook. No rehab and no halfway house this time.

Sentenced to one year, Brandon felt suicidal. They always asked that too, the nurse would come in and ask the inmates: "are you feeling suicidal?" Brandon never felt it before that day. Usually, he never got anything more than a slap on the wrist, so this was a bunch of firsts for him. He was not sure who would actually admit to being suicidal if they really wanted to take their own life.

Brandon certainly was not going to admit to being suicidal he did not want to end up in a turtle suit being watched 24/7. Even using the bathroom. Being watched on the toilet sounded worse than death to him.

So, he kept his mouth shut. Plotting and planning the way he would kill himself. Counting the minutes between cell passes and flashlight checks in the night, he began a journal. A journal with tallies only. No verbiage. Knowing they would read it during cell checks. Nobody was going to foil his plans.

He planned to watch the officers schedule in prison for at least one month before his attempt. Life sucked on the streets, and now it sucked even more doing a year in prison. He had enough.

The first two weeks in prison were not that bad. He was taught how to make jailhouse burritos and how to make a cake from everyday tray items. He even learned how to play cards. Making a few new acquaintances, he seemed to adjust well.

Good I look unsuspecting. He thought to himself as he walked with his coffee up to his card buddy's table.

"Morning guys. Cards early today?" Brandon asked.

"Yeah, as long as you got the first round of coffee." His card pal said.

It had been their tradition for the last couple weeks that one of the gentlemen would make everyone coffee for the morning round of cards. Each day they switched roles, and it went on that way for two weeks. Brandon liked it, he did not feel used or taken advantage of the way some of the other less reputable inmates made him feel.

The day finally came, and Brandon grabbed his thermal pajama set given to him by his recently released cellmate.

Making his way to the shower, unrushed. Acting natural and happy seemed more important today than ever. Placing his cup of coffee at the table with the deck of cards they used daily. To reserve their table. It was the unspoken way of reserving a table – placing personal items on it that nobody wanted to steal.

He started the shower by pressing the button while fixing his thermal pants around his neck as tight as he could stand. Then he tied the thermal pants to the shower head, while intermittently pressing the button to keep the shower running.

Placing his book on the floor standing it up on its vertical edge, gave himself at least 8 inches to prop himself. He stood carefully on the book while tightening the thermals even more.

Kicking the book down while simultaneously pressing the water button, he began to get dizzy and weak. He knew the end was coming. Silent joy washed over him. Finally, he got away from them and his life. He was done. Checking out early.

Depression and anxiety bubbled up in him as sounds began whooshing back in his ears. With his vision blurred he could only make out a brick wall. He groaned. Horribly pissed with himself that his attempt did not work. His eyes finally opened. He looked around.

No shackles, no hospital, no bars. He was shocked for another reason now.

What's going on? He thought as he rubbed his eyes and studied his surroundings.

Looking down, he realized he had been in this spot before. The dumpster. He brushed himself off. Walking towards home, he felt a sense of relief and perplexion. He was not one to look a gift horse in the mouth.

When he arrived on his front porch he attempted to put his key in the door. The lock did not budge.

Knocking frantically on the door, thinking his landlord had changed the locks on him. His landlord came out in a robe and coffee in hand.

"What the hell do you think you're doing?!" She shouted.

"You changed the locks? I wasn't even late this time." Brandon said.

"I don't know you buddy. You better get out of here before I call the police." She slammed the door and watched sternly through the window making sure he left the porch.

Jogging down the street and reaching into his pocket in search for any amount of money, he stopped and found a few crumpled up one's in his pocket.

The nearest coffee shop was close, he would go in there and use their bathroom to get high. Then he planned to sit around and nurse his coffee contemplating what was happening to him.

Looking through the ancient phone book the shop had, he found a local shelter. Figuring this would be a perfect spot to lay low and sleep.

Walking along the city street he could not help but be grateful he was not a ghost or something like that. People could see him and talk to him, he could feel high, and taste coffee.

While he was trudging along trying to make it to the shelter, he looked up and suddenly, there *he* was. Dressed in a suit and tie, shiny shoes, and briefcase in hand. It was *himself*. He stood there staring, watching as this other Brandon walked across the cross walk toward the glass skyscraper.

Holy shit. He thought to himself.

Chasing after himself, but keeping a safe distance, he waited and watched. He saw himself go into the building.

I must work in there. I'm doing pretty good in this life. He chuckled to himself.

There was a bench sitting about a hundred feet from the only entrance to the office building. He would wait and follow himself home.

After what seemed like hours, which was probably only a usual workday, *he* emerged. Same suit, same tie, same briefcase, same shiny shoes. Brandon got up and followed carefully behind.

Man, I must be healthy as a horse here. He thought to himself. Admiring the quick pace at which he was following himself.

Finally, after three blocks of walking, they arrived at the house where this alternate *Brandon* lived.

He had a nice three-story house. Attached like a row home to the next one. Just a little wider.

Yeah, I could live there. Brandon snorted, immediately planning how to get rid of this Brandon and take over his identity.

He hung back, and observed himself, and this new schedule. Brandon would leave and score, come back and get high watching the other Brandon from his backyard.

I know this Brandon has money.

Scheming and conniving were his specialties. He decided to setup a robbery and see if he could kill the new Brandon. Figuring they had the same fingerprints, social, birthdate, and all the other important details to secure money and other assets, he thought it would work perfectly.

After days of watching, it was finally time. Brandon planned to strike. Wrapping his t-shirt around his face, leaving just his eyes, he put his hood up.

He rushed new Brandon coming out of his front door. Soon to be *his* front door.

"Give me everything you got!" Brandon shouted at himself.

"Nice try pal, I hope you're prepared to use that weapon you got. If not. Have a nice day." The other Brandon said while turning to lock his front door.

Damn I don't take any shit in this life either. He thought to himself while steadying his arm.

He shot himself in the back of the head and watched himself topple into the door. He did not even look around to see if anyone saw. He grabbed the keys out of the other Brandon's hands and opened the front door.

Tossing the keys down, he retrieved the body and dragged him inside to bleed out in the back somewhere. Going back out for the briefcase and inspecting for blood, he did a 360 spin around to see if anyone had their nosy faces in the window or watching from a porch. Using his shirt to wipe the spatters of blood of the glass door, he felt confident it looked clean enough.

After being satisfied that nobody saw him, he went back inside and shut all the blinds. Showering in this Brandon's house was the best experience of his life. The last shower he remembered was prison.

He walked around and helped himself to clothes, a snack, and some television. Contemplating on what to do with the body, he decided to just shove himself down into the basement until he could think of a more permanent solution.

Rolling the other Brandon's body down the stairs was easier than he thought it would be. He had wood floors and the body slid across easily. One kick in the back was all it took.

Hearing a knock on the front door jostled him. Closing the basement door, he made his way to the front door.

"Coming!" He shouted.

He waltzed over to the door, undoubtedly higher on substance and power than the dead Brandon had ever been in his entire square life.

Looking through the peephole, he saw a police officer in plain clothes with a badge. Opening the door slowly and standing with his hand on his hip, he waited for the officer to lead.

"Hey Brandon. Everyone at work was worried you didn't show. Unlike you. Something about, it's the first time ever in ten years working there. Wanted me to come by and do a welfare check. What's up with you?" The officer asked.

"I went to a party last night, slept in and forgot to call. Got wrapped up in my own sickness this morning, I guess. I'll call them. Thank you for checking." He said despite wanting to call him a pig, but he knew the other Brandon would never.

Closing the door and getting on the computer that was sitting in the den area, he looked for banking apps and information anywhere. He knew this Brandon had money. He would be endlessly high in this life.

The other Brandon awoke, groggy and stiff. The back of his head felt like he had been bludgeoned. He sat up. Looking around he found himself in the bathroom at work.

Walking out while rubbing the bridge of his nose, he stopped at his admin's desk.

The admin stared at him confused and concerned. "Sir, do you need medical help? Nobody is supposed to be back here unless they have a badge."

"I work here." Brandon said confused.

"You need to leave."

He walked out to the sidewalk and stared at the sky. He had no idea what was going on with him. Digging in his briefcase he dug his phone out and made his way home.

As soon as he got to his stoop, he knew something was really wrong. The curtains were different on the front of the house, and there were plants everywhere.

Cautiously, he inserted his house key into the door. The key was jammed.

What the hell…

"Can I help you?" The woman greeted him over the intercom.

"I'm sorry, how long have you lived here. I think I've mistaken this for my house."

"That's quite alright. We've been here nearly a decade. Do you need medical assistance?"

"No, thank you." Brandon said as he stumbled down the stairs.

Wandering around in search of a place to get a cup of coffee and charge his phone, he paused in his tracks.

Just across the street he spotted *himself*...

Have you ever heard of gay aliens?
How do they reproduce?

Area 69

It was like any other regular day for Trish. Having already met with ten clients she was ready to call it a day. The money was good. Being a high-class escort, she only met with the richest of the rich.

Being dark haired and darker olive skinned, she naturally got the most clients of all the ladies she worked with.

"I'm beat, I'll see you ladies tomorrow." Trish told the other ladies.

"See ya." They said in unison.

Her apartment was just a block from her job. Adding to its lure. Saving money on gas and car insurance really gave her a lot of extra spending money.

The street was dark, and the lights were on above. Her walk home was typical. Pissing homeless people, junkies in alley ways, and stray cats that might be hungry enough to eat a downed junky.

A small stretch of street separated her from her apartment, she could she the front door. A whirring noise that sounded vaguely like a helicopter grew louder above her. Looking up, she saw nothing. The sound grew louder.

"What the hell! Help!" She screamed.

A bright white light gleamed down on her with no apparent originating source. Kicking her heels off and fumbling with her keys, she slammed into her door. Trying desperately to get the key in. It was too late. She was surrounded by white light. Her heels were all that was left of Trish on the street.

"Where the hell am I?" Her voice echoed unnaturally in her own ears.

The entire place was white. It was a circle room, surrounded by doors. No handles. Pushing through the first door she saw creatures folded on top of one another.

I guess animals enjoy 69 too. She thought as she quickly slammed the door.

The next door looked the same. Except this time these creatures most resembled humans. All males. All having sex with each other.

"Hello! What the hell is going on he—?"

Before she could finish a large hand like thing was grabbing her shoulder. Flinging around and preparing to fight, she put her arms up. The thing was hideous. And naked.

It does have a nice dick though. Her eyes travelled from south to north.

"You're in no danger." It said.

"Then what the hell am I doing here in this weird orgy? I'm clearly out of place... if you know what I mean." She said pointing to the doors behind her.

"Precisely." He said grabbing ahold of her with a strength she couldn't even begin to escape from.

Carrying Trish down the hallway, the alien being walked her into a medical room. All the occupants were male. One of them had a mask and was holding a long syringe.

"Oh my god. No! Please!" Trish screamed and clawed and the aliens back.

They laid her down on the table in the center of the room and strapped her legs and arms down.

"Be still or it won't take. The quicker you get this done the quicker you can go back to your hole."

Trish began to sob. She felt the syringe as it touched her cervix. Wincing in pain she screamed out. Her screaming was echoing around her, and she awoke in her own bed.

"Holy shit!" She screamed out loud.

Pawing and patting at her body. She grabbed her full-length mirror and laid down to examine her body in the mirror. Feeling inside herself for any foreign fluids, she found none. Checking her wrists and nails for any signs of ligament marks and alien flesh, she found nothing.

Was I that tired? Am I hallucinating?

Breathless and embarrassed she dressed for work. Putting the incident out of her mind was easy to do when dealing with multiple men during the day. Attributing the awful life-like dream to her line of work was also easy to do. Suspecting a therapist would tell her the same thing, she went on about life like normal.

Being on birth control, Trish thought nothing of missing her period. Usually, she skipped her period on purpose anyway. In her line of work, she wanted as many days available as humanly possible.

It wasn't until the third month of being off her birth control without a period that she grew concerned. Contacting her doctor right away, they were able to get her in.

The doctors drew her blood and tested her urine. They told her she would need to wait a week before her next appointment. Panic stricken, she asked about medical abortion right away.

"Honey, you don't even know if you're pregnant yet. If you're sure about your last menstrual cycle, then you've got plenty of time for an abortion. Just go home and relax and we'll see you next week." The nurse told her.

Easy for you to say. She thought to herself with the images of aliens and syringes flashing in her mind.

I need a drink.

On her way home she stopped and grabbed a bottle of vodka to calm her nerves. Figuring that would help her sleep dreamlessly and kill the images in her mind.

Having induced a drunken sleep, Trish slept soundly for the time in months.

Waiting a week for the next doctor's appointment was like torture for her. Having practically chewed her cheeks raw, she was anxious for the results.

"Trish?" The nurse called her from the waiting room. "Right this way. You'll be in room 4. Just go ahead and get undressed the doctor will be right in."

Doing as instructed, she undressed and sat on the cold papered examine table. The doctor came in no more than five minutes later. The quickest a doctor has ever seen her.

"Trish, hello. I'm Doctor Sinh. How are you feeling?" He asked while looking at her chart not at her.

"Fine."

"Looking over your labs and chart we noticed a few abnormalities and irregularities that require more testing."

"Well, am I pregnant or not? I want an abortion!" Trish raised her voice unintentionally.

"We're not sure. There is something in there. We need to do more tests. The pregnancy tests all came back negative, but the ultrasound shows something. Maybe a mass, maybe nothing serious. Can you come back Friday for a biopsy?"

"Yes, anything. I just need answers."

Leaving the office feeling more concerned about her mental health then she ever had in life. She made her regular stop at the liquor store. Vodka in heavy dosages. That was all the medicine she needed.

On her walk home with her bottle of vodka she felt a cramp in her side. Slowing herself down and taking a breather for a second, she looked to the sky panicked. Feeling like she was being followed, she began to speed walk.

Not being able to shake the feeling of being watched and followed she began to sprint. Pushing her key in the door, she rushed in and slammed it shut. Pressing her back against the door, she caught her breath before putting her eye to the peek hole. She saw nothing. Nobody was following her.

You're really working yourself up.

Twisting the top from her vodka, she poured herself a shot and tipped it down her throat. She poured another.

Feeling a cramp in her side, she doubled over in pain. She felt a trickling warm liquid flow down her leg.

I'm not crazy, it's fricking happening!

Grabbing her purse, she dumped the contents all over the counter. Feverishly searching for her cellphone. Looking up her doctor's number she called him immediately.

"Doctor Sinh's office." The receptionist answered.

Her cheery voice instantly pissed Trish off.

"I have a liquid running down my leg. It's Trish Ingle from earlier today. The doctor needed to run more tests. My pregnan—"

"Please wait a minute I'm grabbing the doctor right now."

"Hurry up, it's hurting! I think there's a baby coming out!"

"Trish, it's Dr. Sinh. You need to hangup with us and call 911 immediately for an ambulance. I'm going to meet you at the hospital."

Heeding her doctor's advice, Trish got on the phone with 911 immediately.

"Police, ambulance, or fire?"

"Ambulance! I'm having an alien baby!" She shouted.

"Are you home?" The operator asked.

"Yes, my address is 118 Coble Street apartment 1. Please hurry!"

"Ma'am you need to get into your bathtub and wait there on your elbows and your knees. Breath in through your nose and out your mouth."

Trish got into her bathtub and bent down. Putting her phone on speaker phone and leaving the operator on the toilet. All she could do was scream and groan in pain.

Blood was pooling under her, and it smelled rancid. Like death.

"They're about five minutes away from you now. Are you still there?" The operator was asking her from the toilet.

Trish screamed in agony as the slippery body of a little alien boy plopped out and into the tub. Its eyes were wide open staring at her. There was no umbilical cord. There was no crying.

A loud whirring noise was growing louder above her again. The bright white light was hovering above her again.

"No! No! Please not again!" Trish screamed.

"Are you still there? The ambulance is at your front door." The operator said.

The white light engulfed the alien baby and Trish. The operator's words were echoing incoherently all around here.

Trish fainted in the tub surrounded by blood and mucus like liquid.

When the EMT's made it to her, she was almost lifeless. Having lost a lot of blood. They rushed her to the hospital. Searching the house, trash cans, and toilet, they were shocked to find no baby. No placenta or any afterbirth at all. Just blood.

Trish awoke screaming. "Where am I?"

"You're at the hospital. Do you remember what happened before you got here?" The emergency room doctor was leaning over her.

"Where is my doctor? Doctor Sinh was supposed to meet me here." Trish asked looking around the room for her doctor.

"He's on his way still. Trish, where is the baby?"

"The aliens. They came back for it." She shouted deliriously.

The doctor and two nurses looked at each other. One of them was already filling out psychiatric papers for commitment.

"I know how it sounds. The aliens abducted me three months ago. They were gay. They were all men. They used a syringe to inject me. I had their baby. They came back for it!" She cried.

Nobody believed her. They stared at her like she was insane. She stopped talking until her doctor arrived.

"You all can think I'm crazy all you want. My doctor will back me up. He wanted to run tests, he knew something weird was going on. Just wait!"

Doctor Sinh arrived and shut the door. "Trish. Tell me what happened."

She retold her story from the beginning. He stared at her, unphased by what he was hearing.

"Trish. If you're going to get out of here, we need to get your story straight." He said to her.

"But…that *is* the story." Trish cried. "You have to believe me. You saw my tests yourself!"

"Of course I believe you. I'm the one who suggested your womb in the first place. It's a great one. Now, the story is… You thought you were pregnant after miscarrying in my care three years ago. The trauma responses can be intense. You thought you were having the baby. The symptoms presented as birth. You convinced yourself and the result was an anxiety attack in the bathroom. Got it? Unless you want them to submit those committal forms to psych today?"

"But why?" She whispered.

"They're an all-male species. How else would they reproduce?"

Reality is subjective… Right?

Mirror Mirror

KNOCK KNOCK KNOCK

A loud pounding on the door woke Tena and Cal out of their sleep.

"Who on earth could that be at this hour?" Tena asked her husband startled and shaking his arm.

"I'll check. You wait here." He said as he flung the blankets from his body and walked down the hall briskly.

He reached the door and looked through the peek hole. Just as he feared…the police. He ran to the kitchen. Ripping the bottom plate off the refrigerator, he grabbed his 9mm. He ran back into the bedroom.

"I love you Tena, no matter what they said I did. I loved you! Stay away from the mirror, it's evil! No matter what!"

"Cal what are you talking about?" She shouted as she jumped from the bed.

When she saw him put the gun into his mouth, she lunged at his legs. Screaming a shrill and horrid scream. She heard the front door bash down.

"Cal no!" She wrestled her way to his waist.

POP

Cal's blood and brain matter splattered the wall behind his head while spraying her in the face. Shaking with terror as she watched his body thump to the back wall and slide down like a scene from a cheesy horror movie. Only this was no horror movie. This was her life. She sat there, crumpled with her hands on his legs, shaking profusely and too stunned to cry.

Without blinking she felt hot tears trail down her cheeks. Smelling sulfur and copper was all she remembered. With ringing in her ears, she heard nothing else.

Feeling the police officers' hands around her arms as they picked her up and brought her into the night air. The cold air assaulted her bare skin through her thin pajamas. She was still sitting on the edge of the police cruiser when the emergency staff was hauling Cal's body away. Trembling and staring at the scene around her as the police voices began to infiltrate her quiet space.

"Ma'am, can you hear me? My name is officer Robins, do you know where you are?" He said as if talking to someone who was from a foreign country with a small light beaming into her eyes. "Guys, take her to the hospital too, I think she's in shock, but we need a witness statement." He backed off and let the emergency crew take over.

He would not get a statement from Tena. Tena would not speak again for the next 6 months. Detective Robbins retired shortly thereafter. Tena would be in the dark about everything leading up to that fateful night.

It had been one year since Cal's suicide. She had a quaint little studio apartment in the basement of Cal's mother's house.

Catherina was the only family she had left now. Knowing Cal would have wanted her to remain close to his mother, she moved in shortly after her hospital stay.

"Tena, I was thinking… you're young and beautiful, you should be dating again. Cal would've wanted you to be happy." Catherina said sweetly.

"I just feel like when the time is right and when I'm not really looking it'll happen. You know?"

"I understand believe me, that's why I'm still alone harping on you. Advice I didn't plan to take myself. I never looked again after Henry. I probably never will." She patted Tena's shoulder and left her there with her thoughts.

As Tena sat in the quiet summer night. She saw a shooting star and the memory of that night came back to her.

Stay away it's evil! She heard booming in her memory.

She practiced her grounding techniques for panic attacks.

The air is cold. The sky is dark. I smell dewy grass and pine. The vines are beautiful.

When she felt her anxiety quell, she opened her eyes slowly.

The next morning, she awoke to the smell of percolating coffee and breakfast. This morning was her meeting with a detective at the sheriff's office to get the information on Cal's case.

Gathering her hair in a bun, she shuffled to the basement stairs. When she placed her foot on the first step of the stairs, she heard a skuttling noise in the storage space underneath. Backing her foot off the step, she went around to the little half door.

Struggling at first to turn the old nob. With a creak, it eventually loosened, and the door opened. She pulled the tattered old string to the dingy lightbulb that was dangling by a thread.

Peering inside she saw a furry mess on the floor. Like a scuffle had ensued between two mice and one lost, horribly. An old mirror was propped against the back of the closet. A gorgeous bulky frame with wooden roses that looked hand crafted. It was a gorgeous antique. When she got back from the police station, she made note to take it to her vanity. It was too heavy to move and get all sweaty now.

The two of them enjoyed a nice breakfast before her appointment with the sheriff. Catherina offered up kind words of encouragement as she always had. Catherina had never inquired into her son's suicide. Maintaining the "I don't need to know the *why* because he's a peace now" mindset seemed so peaceful. Something Tena wished she had.

She arrived 20 minutes before her appointment with the detective. This was a new detective, and he was not in the department while her husband was being investigated. She knew he had the files but the officer she really wanted to speak to was long gone.

"Good morning, Tena, I'm detective Reynolds, and I'll be going over your husbands file with you if you want to follow me this way." He said as he started walking.

Following wordlessly through a secured door to a long stark hallway marked with doors on both sides.

"Alright, would you like any coffee, tea, or water before we start?" he asked.

"No, thank you." She said tucking her purse in her lap.

"First off, I'd like to express my deepest condolences and tell you that your husband is still considered innocent until proven guilty even in death. So, anything we speak about today is in my least judgment."

She believed him. "Thanks. My first question is, what was he being arrested for in the first place?"

"Murder. His file reads: Cal Harrington is accused of murdering Wallace Patrick in the basement of Wallace's home. They were arguing over property. Wallace allegedly had something that belonged to Cal according to a neighbor. Upon searching the house, they found a shard of glass with DNA that matched Cal's. Suspecting he stabbed Wallace to death. The neighbor saw him leaving the home within hours of the time of death estimation from the autopsy report." He read from the case file.

"What was the property that belonged to Cal?"

Disbelieving that her husband was capable of such things. Especially such a close, and messy means of murder. Shock came over her again.

"We still don't know. Nobody who knew them could elaborate. The neighbor insisted it was a mirror the pair had been arguing about, some antique. This hasn't been substantiated."

Sitting rigid in the chair and feeling a slow prickle come over her legs, forcing the fresh shaved leg hairs out back into the world. She felt weak.

"Interesting." She said, careful to keep composed. "I didn't know of any missing items from our home, and it never became a topic of conversation between us."

"Did he say anything before his suicide Tena?" He asked in a quieter more sensitive tone.

"No." She lied.

"Well, if there is nothing else, I can escort you to the front." He offered as he closed the file and slid it to the side.

"I think that's all I needed today for some closure. Thank you for your time."

The detective ushered her down the same hallway and back to the secured door. "Have a good day, Tena, nice meeting you, and my condolences again." He said with a slight head nod.

She walked quickly to her car with a ringing in her ears that threatened to drown out the world.

The sun is shining. I hear birds chirping. I see grass. I feel the sun's rays on my skin.

After the episode of anxiety passed, she started her car and began the trek back home.

When she got back, she told Catherina she was not feeling hungry. Heading straight for the basement to dig through her husband's packed up things. She knew he was hiding something now.

The boxes were dusty and smelled of musty basement. After pawing through about six boxes, she was growing tired. Determination wouldn't let her stop though. Opening the seventh box she discovered what looked like old encyclopedias.

Just as she was closing the box back up something about one of the books numbered 8 stuck out to her. There, next to the 8 was and "x" engraved in the leather-bound spine of the book.

Tena pulled the book out and blew the dust from the edges. When she opened the book, she was shocked when she realized that it was not an encyclopedia, but a journal. Yet another thing she did not know about Cal. She had no idea he liked to journal.

The dates were a few weeks before his suicide. So, she grabbed a cup of coffee from upstairs and went back down into the seclusion of the basement to start reading her husband's journal.

Entry One:

When I found it, I knew I needed to put it up in the house for Tena to enjoy. I wanted to restore it to glory. I brought it out to my workstation in the garage. When I stood over it, rag in hand and ready to wipe it clean. It started up like a show on T.V. It showed me a promotion at work, although not the date, just a promotion and ceremony. My gosh did that feel good seeing that! I stood there compelled to clap myself. When I realized that I was smiling too big and compelled to clap at a hallucination I threw the rag down on the glass and left the mirror in that spot for two days. It was on the morning of the second day when I walked into the office and my boss had planned a nice lunch. Ruby was the gossiping type and liked to be the first to "place a bug in someone's ear." She let me know my boss had promotion plans for someone. I was faint. I knew it was not for me, because what had I done beside show up at work and do what is asked of me? Naturally, I went to my desk and carried out a normal morning only to be flabbergasted that I was the one called out in front of all my peers for promotion. It was exactly as I saw in the mirror. Too shocked to speak, my boss spoke for me. I was grateful but excited to leave and get home to my mirror to find out what else it had in store for me. The afternoon crawled by painfully. When I could punch out, I practically broke every speed limit getting home to it. The mirror. I know, it's just a mirror, but this mirror saw the future. Or did it create the future? I will come back and write the next prediction that it has.

Tena was stunned. She felt compelled to go look more closely at the mirror in the stairwell. Setting her coffee mug down and walking to the staircase like a million dollars lay in wait.

The door creaked open, she tugged the tattered string, and the light bulb illuminated the exact mirror from Cal's journal. As she touched it gingerly, she felt the sanding marks, although the roses were not all black, two were, and the white trim was started but clearly not finished.

Walking into the closet and ducking to avoid hitting her head on the steps, she peered into the mirror. What she saw was like a scene from a movie. It was her on the news talking with a reporter. Unable to hear the words, she read the banner under the news anchor, "live at 9, choking patron saved by ex-patient."

Tripping backward out of the closet she nearly ripped the light bulb and string out of the ceiling. She grabbed her husband's journals and decided to binge read them now that she believed him.

Entry Two:

Today when I got back home, I took the mirror out of hiding and looked again. I saw something horrible. The mirror showed my wife being chased down an alley way near her favorite coffee shop. I recognized it immediately. I was close to seeing the assailant when Tena fell to the ground. I can hardly make out the man's profile. I walked away from the mirror and came back to look a few minutes later. Nothing more of the attacker was revealed. I came back to the mirror after some hours, just to find the same awful scene play out. I felt so helpless. Tomorrow, I will watch that alley way and set up a hidden camera to watch and see who this attacker is.

Entry Three:

The next day instead of going to the office, I went to the alley way and used my memory to set up a camera in the spot that would capture his face. That day I bit my nail beds to bloody pulps in anticipation.

I couldn't wait to get home to sit in front of the mirror again and see what new things were revealed about this predator. I had to stop him before he got Tena. I saw nothing on my phone for days. I won't tell Tena. She will think I'm insane or be scared of me.

Entry Four:

I saw his face! And I found someone on the dark web to help me use facial recognition to find the bastard. I am determined to find him. I will find him. I shelled out whatever sum of money the man who went by "D.J" on the dark web was asking to use my video to give this face a name. $1,000. A small price to pay for Tena's life I thought. He told me his name. Wallace Patrick and that was it. It was up to me to find his address after all that money. I wasn't going to complain because I was happy to have a name. As I write this, I'm actively searching all social medias for this guy.

Entry Five:

I found Wallace. He lives in a neighborhood just a five minutes' walk from Tena's coffee shop (yes, I timed it). I stood outside and confirmed it. It's him. I am planning a confrontation. I'm not sure how yet, but I plan on it. I will watch for a few more days when I can get away without arousing Tena's suspicions.

Tena was unsure what to think.

It's true then. He was a murderer.

She put a bookmark in his hidden journal and brought it to bed with her. Having already made up her mind that she forgave him and whatever led him to murder. It was clear to her now, he was protecting her.

Her dreams were flashbacks of his suicide and his last words to her that night. Marked by tossing and turning, her sleep was fitful and restless. Being clammy and uncomfortable woke her up before the sun.

"Good morning you look well rested and bright eyed today." Catherina said in her usual early morning cheer.

Incredible, because I don't feel it!

"Good morning."

Catherina fixed them breakfast silently, trying to respect Tena's quiet morning. Catherina usually disappeared in the house after cooking to do whatever she did all day.

Tena was thinking of applying for work at the dry cleaners in town. Needing something to occupy her time and contribute to the bills. The dry cleaners would be a nice quiet job.

Resume in hand, Tena took off for town.

The dry cleaner building was small. It had a cozy lobby with soft lighting. When Tena walked in the front door, the owner was there facing her.

"Good morning, I noticed a help wanted sign out front and I thought I would drop in. My name is Tena Harrington I have my resume and wondered if you would consider me for the job?"

"Good morning Ms. Harrington, I am Maryann Teal. It's nice to meet you. I haven't had much traffic in here for the position. Of course I would consider! Why don't you swing around this way to my office and I'll you get you the standard forms. You like tea?"

"Absolutely, any tea."

As the ladies rounded the corner, they passed the moving rack of dry-cleaned clothes. The kitchen was on the left, and a peek through window overlooking the lobby was on the right. She could see a man standing in the lobby looking at the notices on the wall.

Maryann's office was a gorgeous mix of deep rich cherry wood and blood red velvets.

"Wow, it's luxurious in here. Beautiful office."

"Thank you, I spend most my days here why not be comfortable right? My late husband did most of the woodwork." She said.

"Industrious man it seems."

"Very much." She said as she turned and plugged the K-cup into the Keurig machine to make some tea. "Black? Or you like cream and sugar?"

"Oh, black is fine thank you."

"Tell me about yourself Tena, why the rinky dink dry cleaners?"

"I consider it cozy, not rinky dink. The job seems right up my alley because I used to starch and press all my husband's clothes before he passed. I learned from his mother. I have always considered myself organized and clean. And truthfully, I have not worked since my husband passed away and this is just what I need to get into society again while also helping my mother-in-law." Tena explained.

"To be honest with you, I don't even need a formal application. I will take the resume and we'll get everything set for next Monday morning. How does that sound?" She asked with a feeble wink that had a slight shake to her eye.

"It sounds amazing, and I won't be able to express enough gratitude!"

"Well let's walk around back. The grand tour."

The ladies were headed to the back and passed the peek through window again. The man who Tena saw looking at the bulletin board with notices on it was clutching his throat and turning blue. Tena reacted without thinking. Leaping through the small window and grabbing the man from behind, she began to thrust her fists in his chest.

Maryann shouted, "He's choking!" while she burst through her office door searching for her telephone to call 911.

Tena stepped behind the man and just as he went deeper blue and limp, she dislodged the foreign object. It went flying across the lobby. The man fell forward into the wall. Tena struggled to get him down to the floor to complete the CPR.

Maryann rushed back in on the phone with the 911 dispatch trying to relay mouth to mouth resuscitation. Within minutes, two EMT's were rushing in. They had a stretcher and rushed the man out.

Maryann tossed her keys and told Tena to lock up. Too stunned to even move from the spot she just stood there. Exhausted both mentally and physically. She locked up and made her way home.

Catherina was already cooking. She could see her standing in front of the stove from the driveway. Tena did her best to straighten up before heading inside. She already knew that she was obviously frazzled and disheveled.

"Are you alright? You look pale honey" Catherina said as soon as she laid eyes on Tena.

"I saved a man from choking to death today." She said while looking past her at the pots on the stove simmering vigorously.

"That's fantastic, you're a hero and a lifesaver Tena! Let's celebrate with the good wine tonight, what do you say? I know it must have been difficult with all you have been through but let's put a positive spin on it tonight, okay?"

Yes, because there is no way I recognize that man. The mirror could not have been right about that, it was not any doctor I had at the hospital. I'm sure of it. And I wasn't on the news.

"You're right." She sighed. "Let's celebrate. What's on the menu?"

"You're in luck! I made some pot roast with mashed potatoes. Freshen up and I'll call you when it's ready."

Tena cautiously made her way down the stairs. She turned to the closet under the stairs instead of the bedroom. Turning on the light and stepping inside, she looked into the mirror. While looking into the mirror, the news came up and the man from the dry cleaners was on the T.V. this time.

How can this be?

Turning the light off and slamming the door. The thought of smashing the damn thing crossed her mind.

When they sat down to eat Tena requested they watch the news. The news anchors continued throughout their meal. Sure enough, 30 minutes after the top stories.

"And for tonight's special spotlight; former nurse Ray at Memorial Hope needed saving today while eating a snack in the lobby of a dry cleaner. Tonight, we head over to Brad with the story. Brad?"

Tena could not believe her ears. She dropped her fork and fumbled for the remote to turn it up. Catherina paused mid forkful and spun around to watch the story.

"Well Bridget, it's a harrowing story of the savior needing saving. After leaving his shift at Memorial Hope psychiatric hospital, Ray went to pick up his clothes here, at a local dry cleaner. In a twist of fate, the nurse's former patient who he recognized immediately and will go unnamed for privacy reasons, saved his life. A bizarre coincidence that Ray attributes to karma. Ray has made a full recovery and plans to seek the ex-patient out for a personal thank you. How touching right? Back you Bridget."

The news flipped back to the anchor woman seated in the studio and Tena could not even hear. Her ears were ringing too loud.

The next morning Tena decided she would break the stupid mirror and be done with it. Honestly, she was afraid of it.

How could it know what's going to happen?

Grabbing her husband's journal, she walked into the stairwell, and opened the closet door. The mirror sat there in the dark, looming. Taking a few steps back, she flung her husband's journal with all her strength straight at the mirror. The shards flew and scattered to pieces around her. As she went to grab the broom she heard some tinkling noises.

Frozen with fear with each little clink and ting. She stood silent and her mouth hung open in disbelief as she watched the shards of the mirror sticking straight up, pointing to the ceiling. The shards of glass started flying towards her, and she felt her skin puncturing and piercing. Her stomach was on fire. Not sure what was happening until she looked down and saw blood and stab wounds all over. Blood was dripping to her feet.

As she struggled to breathe, she watched the mirror put itself back together piece by bloody piece. Clutching her bloody wounds, she noticed her husband's journal had flopped open to the page she left off on. Coincidentally his last entry before committing suicide. As she lay dying and bleeding out, she scooted over to the journal.

Entry Six:

It's evil! The devil. I'll be blamed, and I have no way to prove my suspicions. I will rot in prison for this. I confronted Wallace. I made him look into the mirror to see his disgusting and vile plan against my wife. He looked and cheered. I became irate. I smashed the mirror to pieces at his feet and slapped him. We both heard the mirror begin to pull its broken shards to the center of the room. The glass started flying and assaulting us both. I shielded myself by shoving Wallace in the way. After all, he was planning to murder my wife! Wasn't he? I saw it! I ran outside and investigated the basement window and saw Wallace... Dead in a pool of blood. The most insane part of this was that the mirror put itself back together. Piece by piece with blood still trailing all over it! I went back inside to take the evil thing. I put it in my mother's basement. I am afraid to burn it, what will happen to me, or to the house? I can't bear another person getting hurt. It sounds crazy. I know it does. I know they will come for me. I'll tell Tena about this, before they come. I'll warn her. I can't live with myself for allowing her to think I am capable of murder

Tena lay dying in a pool of her own blood, while the mirror lay unbroken, full of blood.

If it is evil, just cry out in the name of Jesus.
…I think that's how it works.

The Attic

Lisa and John found the perfect spot for their family. They had been searching tirelessly for months, eight to be specific, for the perfect home.

Lisa had a laundry list of qualities the new house had to possess. John acted like he was just along for the ride. He handled all the finances; she was the one to raise the questions and demands. They got lucky with the Victorian style home they found. The house was historic and had so much character, it was all the things Lisa wanted. Well within budget too.

Moving day was a chaotic day for the whole family. The movers were late, the boxes were placed in the wrong rooms. The kids did not seem to care though because all three of them had their rooms picked out months ago.

It was their first night in the new place and even though all her kids were above the age of seven, Lisa still worried about them and if they were alright to be alone. She offered her bed to each one of the kids and they all declined.

The youngest of the bunch was Maria, she was 8 going on 18. She was sassy and was not afraid to show it. She loved all things barbie and pink, she wanted the pink drapes, the pink canopy bed, the whole bit.

Maxwell was the middle child, he had middle child syndrome. He often told silly lies and pulled pranks. When he was younger, he was often told the story of the boy who cried wolf to reiterate the importance of truth telling and knowing when to be serious and when to kid around.

The oldest of the bunch was Alex, he was stubborn and very independent. As an early teen he was getting more defiant and isolated. He was bright and gifted, hitting every milestone early from infancy.

Lisa was proud of her kids and could go on for hours discussing them if allowed. They were a good bunch, and she felt such joy going to bed that night knowing her kids were in a better place and bigger space.

"You want to break the new place in?" John asked in a suggestive tone.

She knew what that meant and gosh did he look good signing for the house. Thanks to him they had a house to break in. With just a mattress on the floor, it should be quiet enough, she reasoned.

When morning came there was no real groceries to cook, so they made the trek to the charming diner down the street.

"The parking lot is crowded… that's always a good sign." John said as he looked in the rearview mirror to make sure the kids shared his enthusiasm.

They rarely did these days. They were at the age where nothing a parent says is ever cool.

They occupied the window seat. John insisted, so he could watch his car. That was their regular decision-making process when picking a seat in a restaurant. The visibility of the car. Like someone would hop in and drive off if John were not hawking over it.

A woman walked by the window and stared into the diner at the family and their meal. John and the woman made eye contact and he smiled and nodded gently. Smiling too big and staring, she jabbed the glass with the finger, which bent back in an unnatural way.

"All right move along now." John said aloud while motioning her off.

"Honey, she's homeless and hungry just show some compassion. Maybe we can box our food and bring it to her when we're done." Lisa said gently patting his arm to bring it back down.

The family collectively averted their eyes awkwardly back to their own plates.

They walked outside and rounded the building after their breakfast. They were all searching for the woman without success.

Just as soon as John put his arm on the headrest and turned to back out of the parking space, the woman was there behind the car just staring.

"Jesus!" He shouted and put the car back in park. "Give me the food please."

The kids pushed the food up to the front seat and immediately turned around to crane their necks to watch.

"Here ma'am, my kids and I set aside some food for you." He extended the food.

She took the containers in her ripped up gloved hands. "Thank you, and your kids too. I would leave your house if I were you."

"Excuse me?"

"If you love those kids, leave. Weird things happen there. Didn't anyone tell you about the last family?"

"Have a nice day ma'am." He turned to walk away.

"The wife… she went crazy. Hung herself in the attic. The husband killed the kids. He's in prison now."

John reached the car without turning around at all. He pulled out and around the woman who just stood there and stared at their car.

"What in the world was she spouting about?" Lisa asked with a chuckle.

"I think she's mentally ill." John said as he stared straight ahead.

Sunday was always church and a big dinner. Lisa insisted. The kids were starting to resent church. Their friends did not go to church, and they despised having to dress up. John did not care for it much either.

This would be their first time at a new church. John and Lisa were hoping to make meaningful connections and had already been given the names of the couple who would show them around.

"Glad you could make it! I'm Theresa, and this is Abel. It's so great to have you." She shook hands with Lisa and John. "Well, hello there! You must be Maria, Max, and Alex. I have heard such lovely things about you kids. Let me show you to the young adult's room." She said in a tone that was more for babies then the kids standing in front of her.

"If you want to follow me." Abel said to Lisa and John while the kids were ushered off.

He started off with the grand tour of the place and where the notable things were.

"Thanks Abel. We appreciate the warm welcome." Lisa said.

Theresa joined back up and linked arms with Abel before hushing her voice. "Grady down at the diner mentioned a run-in with that homeless woman. She's truly harmless, but she says some blasphemous things. It's best to steer clear of her."

"Yes." John agreed nodding his head.

"You already know you just cry out in the name of Jesus Christ if you have issues in that house. No matter what the history is. Jesus will protect you." Abel whispered.

The house was dark. Everyone was cozied up in their rooms. The clock ticked loudly, and the fan droned on above John's head. He frequently awoke at the same time every night to use the restroom. He was laying silently staring into the dark abyss of the ceiling when he heard a clatter from the kitchen.

A pot and pan clinked together faintly.

He sat up straight and stopped breathing. Holding his breath, hoping to sharpen his ears by not breathing.

The cabinet jostled and he heard the wood bump shut.

He stood up and walked to the top of the stairs staring down at the first floor. Searching the hall closet for anything that would double as a weapon. He saw a container of bleach and grabbed it by the handle.

The steps made creaks and groans as he stepped gingerly on each one. His toes dug into the stairs as he clutched the bleach ready to assault whatever he found.

As he reached the middle of the staircase, he saw a black rat come barreling onto the stairs. Its nails tore into the stairs and made a loud rustling noise as it climbed the stairs. He heaved the bottle of bleach at the rat. Missing its body.

The hallway lights came on and illuminated the staircase.

"Honey are you okay?!" Lisa said gasping.

"Yeah, didn't you see that huge rat come flying by?" He said breathlessly.

"Let's just go back to bed we can call a pest company in the morning."

He followed her back to bed cautiously scouring the baseboards for rats or excrement. Unable to close his eyes, he stared at the ceiling. Lisa began to snore.

Just as he was about to close his eyes and drift into his dreams, he heard scuddling around in the attic. A digging nose was just above them. A feverish scratching and clawing.

"Vermon." He muttered disgusted.

Sleeping fitfully. Dreaming of electrical fires starting in the rat's nest and engulfing the attic is what John's dreams were comprised of. Once he finally fell asleep.

The smell of coffee and breakfast preceded John's alarm that morning. He stretched long and tall before making his way downstairs.

"Good morning beautiful." He said as he embraced Lisa and kissed her.

"Good morning. I hope you got to sleep after that incident last night."

The house was quiet as he gathered his poisons from his boxes in storage. He wrapped his feet in plastic garbage bags and got the best pair of rubber cleaning gloves Lisa owned. Determined to start the pest control himself.

He was unlatching the attic hinges when he noticed a glowing light coming through. Armed with a hammer from his toolbox he readied himself. Creeping up the attic ladder slowly with the hammer raised high, his eyes scanned the floor. Seeing nothing, he proceeded.

He hoisted himself up and in. Being careful around the old rafters. The last thing he needed was to end up crashing through the ceiling into the floor below.

Swatting the cobwebs and moving steadily towards the source of the light. He could see no light switches anywhere. He saw the lightbulb that was hanging on the other side of a large metal unit.

Deciding to unscrew the light since he couldn't find the switch. Placing his hand on the bulb and ripping it back just as fast.

"God damnit!" He shouted as he clutched his pounding, red palm.

The light must have been on for a while because it was hotter than hell.

"You're not supposed to use the Lord's name in vain. Right dad?" Alex shouted up sarcastically from the bottom of the attic steps.

"Alex, why don't you make yourself useful and get me an oven mitt from the kitchen." John said back irritated and in pain.

After unscrewing the lightbulb and spraying poison over the entire perimeter of the attic, John was satisfied with his work.

Later that night, the clock on John's alarm struck 1:11 am. He got up to use the bathroom like he always did. Passing under the square hatch that housed the attic steps he saw a faint light coming from in the attic again.

Impossible. He thought to himself.

Glancing at the lightbulb he had removed from the attic earlier in the day. It was still sitting in the decorative bowl in the hallway.

Trying his best to be quiet, he unlatched the attic stairs. They creaked and groaned the way old wood with metal springs do. He clenched his teeth and cringed with the noises as the steps opened fully.

As he reached the top of the steps, he saw the attic was completely illuminated. He stepped on the other side of the air conditioning unit and this time instead of seeing a lightbulb, there was nothing. Light was coming from the empty spot in which he unscrewed the lightbulb earlier.

Rubbing his eyes and stepping back unaware of his footing and too stunned to pay attention, he stepped on a soft spot. His entire foot broke through the ceiling. Frantically grabbing at anything he could to stop himself from falling all the way through the ceiling.

Finally steadying himself on the metal unit, he hoisted himself upright. Making his way back to the stairs, he practically jumped out of his skin when Lisa appeared at the bottom of the steps.

"John! What are you doing up there at this hour?"

"I was on my way to the bathroom, and I noticed the light was back on in here, but when I got up here, I got freaked out because the lightbulb was taken out. Look for yourself Lis." John said as he turned around and walked back up the steps.

Lisa followed in her night gown.

"John I just really think this could have waited until morning. It's so dangerous up here."

She followed him all the way to the other side of the metal unit. Waiting for John to speak up and narrate for her. He said nothing.

John was flabbergasted once more when he saw a new lightbulb screwed into the hole that was just illuminated moments prior.

"So, is that the lightbulb you said you took out?" Lisa asked.

"Honey, even if I didn't take it out. I turned it *off* and now it's back on. Nobody was up here today. So how did it get turned back on?"

"Can we go to bed now? Jesus, is that a hole?!" She asked, noticing the spot where John's foot had pierced.

"I will fix that."

"He's been acting strange." Lisa told Theresa at church that next Sunday.

"Strange how?" She asked concerned.

"Well, he has been going up into that attic every night at strange hours. He claims every day that he has turned off the light, removed the bulb, and the light keeps finding a way to be turned on. Every night he's investigating."

"Well, if it is an evil spirit, you just cry out in the name of Jesus Christ Lisa."

"I want my husband back. Pray for us, will you?"

"Absolutely."

The family gathered at the table while Maria and Max discussed their day. Maria was excited she got chocolate milk at lunch with spaghetti. It sounded so off putting. Lisa remembered being young and excited about chocolate milk and weird food too. Max talked about the art class project with clay and how he was making himself a mug that he could drink from. Alex was quiet and reserved as usual. Too cool for dinner talks now.

Although none of the kids complimented John on his cooking skills, he knew it was a hit. Chewing and scraping forks was all he heard. The silence and requests for seconds were all the praise he really needed.

After dinner they decided on family movie night. It had been ages since they had one. A loud thud echoed above them as they all decided on a movie. It sounded distant. Lisa and John looked at each other. John froze.

"The attic." He said sullenly.

Everyone froze and stared at John.

"Honey… We'll just call someone."

"No, call who? Jesus Christ?" He asked mockingly.

"Oh John." Lisa scoffed, offended.

"No seriously Lis, think rationally. Something weird is happening. First the homeless woman telling stories of this place, then all the weird stuff happening. You see the way people at church looked at us when we told them where we moved." He was getting more frantic the more he rambled.

"Just calm down. I'll go up there with you so we can rule things out, and tomorrow we call someone. Sound good honey?" She said in her best placating tone.

He did not return the sentiment. He grabbed a knife, a broom, and oven mitts just in case. Then he proceeded to the attic.

Grabbing the hinge and letting the stairs fall in the familiar creaking and groaning tone, the stairs opened fully. Lisa, Max, and Alex followed in a line.

The light was bright. All the family was standing on the rafters except for Maria, she hung back on the top step of the attic stairs. Everyone was in a single file line following John over to the other side of the metal unit. One by one they made their way over.

Everyone looked on in utter shock and fear when they saw the illumination in the attic was not coming from a lightbulb, but an empty space just as John described. Fear began to streak each one's face muddying their features.

"Shh!" Yipped John when Maria started to say something.

"But daddy I hear some—" Silence washed over the top step where Maria occupied just moments ago.

"Maria?!" Yelled Lisa.

Just as the family was following behind Lisa to investigate what happened to Maria a swarm of rats began coming in from the ceiling, insulation, metal unit, and attic steps.

Alex began climbing the metal unit to get off the ground. Lisa tumbled down the attic stairs and subsequently down the stairs below that as well. Max fell to the floor and was overtaken by the swarm of rats. Being ripped and shred to pieces by large teeth. John, attempting to swing a rat off his pant leg, fell backwards through the ceiling and bashing into the tub below. Blood ran from his head and nose, covering the soft white porcelain in a crimson red. Rats hopped down on top of him and began ripping at his clothes and flesh.

Alex lay there motionless on the unit repeating in his mind. *Cry out in the name of Jesus Christ. Cry out in the name of Jesus Christ. Cry out in the name of Jesus Christ.*

When the police arrived at the residence they found the entire family dead except Alex. He was in a state of shock waiting in the attic on top of an air handling unit. The police took him into custody for questioning.

The official report was that the troubled teen had a mental break. Lured his family into the attic. Pushed his little sister and mom down the flight of stairs. Mutilating his entire family into piles of pulp before help arrived.

The only statement Alex gave to police was: "It was evil… I cried out in the name of Jesus Christ, and they still died."

The house went back up for sale, and another horror story was passed around town.

Also by Camille Danciu

Ava

Coming Soon:

On Behalf of all Women

Visit amazon.com/author/camilledanciu for more titles.

Or facebook.com/camille.danciu for future releases and additional information.

Made in the USA
Middletown, DE
09 September 2024